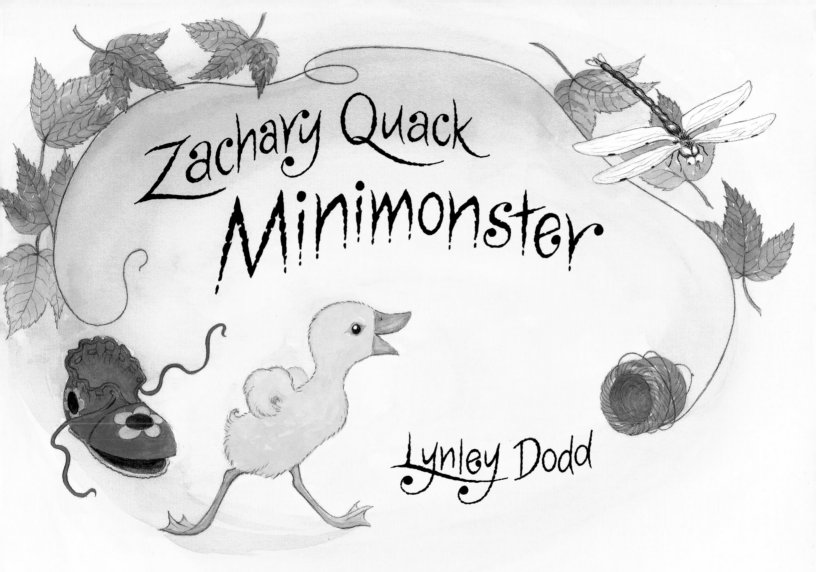

Zachary Quack
Minimonster

Lynley Dodd

PUFFIN BOOKS

Climbing the river bank
on to the track,
went pittery pattery
Zachary Quack.

He scruffled a centipede
out of its house,
he pestered a spider
and ruffled a mouse.

He bustled a beetle
asleep on a chair,
and hustled a dragonfly
into the air.

FLICK
went the dragonfly,
FLICK FLICK FLICK,
here, there and everywhere,
quick,
quick,
quick.

Over the path
and the rockery too,

over some paint
and a bottle of glue.

FLICK
went the dragonfly,
FLICK FLICK FLICK,
here, there and everywhere,
quick,
quick,
quick.

Through the petunias,
pumpkins and peas,

over the rake
and a mountain of leaves.

FLICK
went the dragonfly,
FLICK FLICK FLICK,
here, there and everywhere,
quick,
quick,
quick.

Over the sandpit,
around the old swing,

the netting and potting mix,
tied up with string.

FLICK
went the dragonfly,
FLICK FLICK FLICK,

back to the river bank,
quick,
quick,

PUFFIN BOOKS

Published by the Penguin Group
Penguin Books Ltd, 80 Strand, London WC2R 0RL, England
Penguin Group (USA) Inc., 375 Hudson Street, New York, New York 10014, USA
Penguin Group (Canada), 10 Alcorn Avenue, Toronto, Ontario, Canada M4V 3B2 (a division of Pearson Penguin Canada Inc.)
Penguin Ireland, 25 St Stephen's Green, Dublin 2, Ireland (a division of Penguin Books Ltd)
Penguin Group (Australia), 250 Camberwell Road, Camberwell, Victoria 3124, Australia (a division of Pearson Australia Group Pty Ltd)
Penguin Books India Pvt Ltd, 11 Community Centre, Panchsheel Park, New Delhi - 110 017, India
Penguin Group (NZ), cnr Airborne and Rosedale Roads, Albany, Auckland 1310, New Zealand (a division of Pearson New Zealand Ltd)
Penguin Books (South Africa) (Pty) Ltd, 24 Sturdee Avenue, Rosebank, Johannesburg 2196, South Africa

Penguin Books Ltd, Registered Offices: 80 Strand, London WC2R 0RL, England

www.penguin.com

Published in New Zealand by Mallinson Rendel Publishers Limited 2005
Published in Great Britain in Puffin Books 2005
1 3 5 7 9 10 8 6 4 2

Copyright © Lynley Dodd, 2005

The moral right of the author/illustrator has been asserted

Manufactured in China

British Library Cataloguing in Publication Data
A CIP catalogue record for this book is available from the British Library

ISBN 0-141-38188-4